TERROR IN T

At Claw School Dojo:

Hiro, I must send you, Naga, Tora, and Rashi to find the next Power Jade.

Power Jade Bravery?

Yes. It is hidden in the caves of Mount Kamado.

Evil Master Gomi will try to stop you with Fear Spells.

JUST IN TIME

At Claw School Dojo:

I failed.

You did not get the jade, but you did not fail.

Where are Naga, Tora, and Rashi?

They are not back yet?

What happened?

They ran from a Fear Spell.

And you?

I tried to be brave as you told me.

RAID FOR THE JADE